Daddies Do It Too

La Williams
Toni Crossman

I sit at the table as I play with my breakfast with my fork.

"What's wrong Gene?" My older sister, Genelle asks.

"Today is family day at school. Most of my peers live with their mom and dad, some just live with their mom, and some even live with their grandparents- but I'm the only one who lives with my dad- just my dad."

"So?"

"So I'm the weird one in the class," I complain.

"You're not weird Gene, our family is just different. Our dad does exactly what all of those other parents do."

I think about everything my dad does for Genelle and I.

My dad wakes me up for school every morning. He makes sure I brush my teeth and shower before helping me pick out the perfect- most coolest outfit.

My dad fixes us breakfast and he always says, "Breakfast is the most important meal of the day!"

Sometimes he lets us help him make breakfast.

Dad watches us get on the bus, I'm in first grade and go to elementary school.

Genelle is in eighth grade and goes to middle school.

Once we're on the bus, he goes to work.
Dad is an architect- he designs and builds houses
and buildings.

Dad always promises to get home early, but most nights Genelle and me eat dinner without him- usually a dinner he prepared the night before.
"Just put the oven on 350 and let it cook for about an hour," he usually says.

No matter what, Dad always comes into my room and says goodnight to me when he gets home.

When me or Genelle is sick, Dad stays up with us.
He gives us medicine and soup.

When we are sad, Dad gives us reassuring hugs and promises us that things will get better.

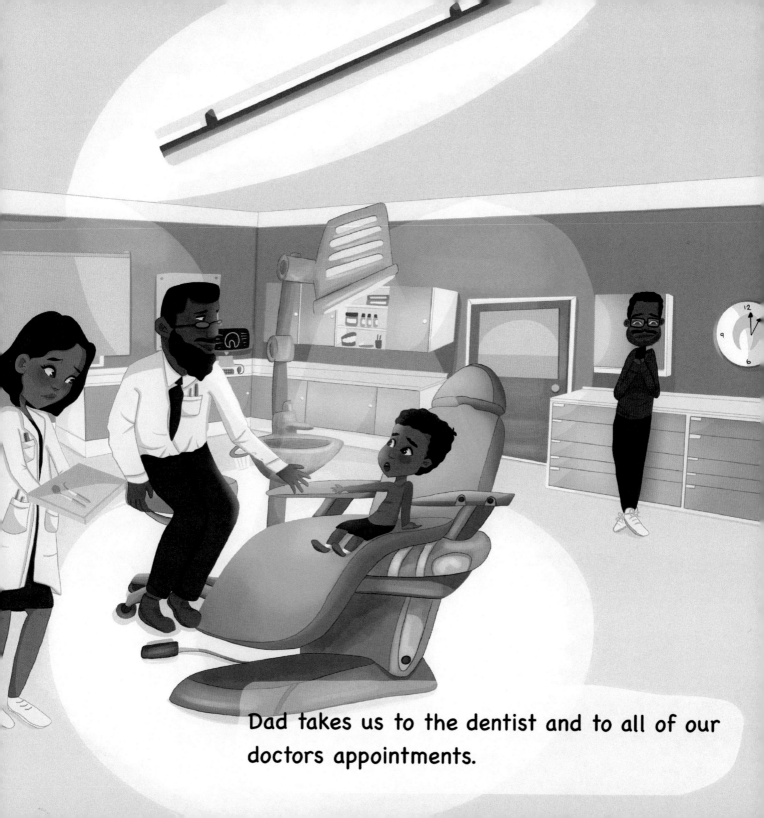

Dad takes us to the dentist and to all of our doctors appointments.

Dad takes us to the movies, museums, parks, and zoos!
Once a year, we even take a vacation!

Last year we stayed at a beach house in Florida.

Every other week, we get to visit our Mom. Sometimes Mom calls to cancel and that makes me sad and Dad angry. Genelle always says, "I don't care," but I know she really does.

Mom lives on the other side of town.

Dad drops us off on a Friday and we stay with Mom until Monday morning- she takes us to school, but after school we ride the bus back home.

I smile as I snap out of my daydream.
I look at Genelle- she is smiling too.
"You're right Genelle!" I say.
"Daddies do, do it too! I can't wait to go to school to share my story."

The End

LaQuesha 'LA' Williams was born and raised in the Midwest. She became a published author for the first time when she was in second grade. Williams is a graduate of Indiana University. She is a grade school teacher in her hometown of South Bend, Indiana. The "I'm Just Like You,"author writes to make a difference in the lives of her readers. She wants her books to have a positive impact on the lives of all those that read her books.

Toni Rose Crossman was born and lives in the United Kingdom with her two children and partner. She has been working as an illustrator for 3 years and this is the second book she's worked on with LA Williams illustrating "I'm Just Like You"
Toni took great inspiration from her own children's relationship with their dad when illustrating this book.

Made in the USA
Monee, IL
11 October 2021